SpongeBob Goes to the Doctor

by Steven Banks
based on a teleplay written by Paul Tibbitt, Ennio Torresan Jr., and Mr. Lawrence
illustrated by Zina Saunders

SIMON SPOTLIGHT/NICKELODEON
New York   London   Toronto   Sydney

Stephen Hillenburg

Based on the TV series *SpongeBob SquarePants*® created by Stephen Hillenburg as seen on Nickelodeon®

 SIMON SPOTLIGHT

An imprint of Simon & Schuster Children's Publishing Division
1230 Avenue of the Americas, New York, New York 10020

Manufactured in the United States of America
10 9 8 7 6 5 4 3
ISBN-13: 978-1-4169-0359-8
ISBN-10: 1-4169-0359-3

SpongeBob woke up one morning feeling terrible. "Oh, Gary, I don't feel like myself," said SpongeBob. "AH-CHOO!" When SpongeBob sneezed, pink bubbles blew out of all his holes.

"Meow," said Gary.

"Don't be silly, Gary," said SpongeBob. "I don't have a cold. I don't get colds, I get the suds."

"Meow," Gary replied.

"No! I can't get the suds!" cried SpongeBob. "Then I'd have to miss work, and I can't miss a day of working at the Krusty Krab!"

"SpongeBob, what's holding up those Krabby Patties?" yelled Mr. Krabs.
"Coming right up, sir," said SpongeBob, sniffling.

Mr. Krabs poked his head through the window. "What's wrong with you, boy? You're paler than a baby sea horse! Do you have the suds?"

"No, sir!" said SpongeBob weakly. "I feel great! AH . . . AH . . . AH-CHOO!"

"SpongeBob, you're too sick to work," said Mr. Krabs. "Go home and get some rest."

"No, Mr. Krabs," said SpongeBob, pleading. "I'm okay! Honest!"

"Nothing personal, lad," said Mr. Krabs. "But I can't have you sneezing all over my food!"

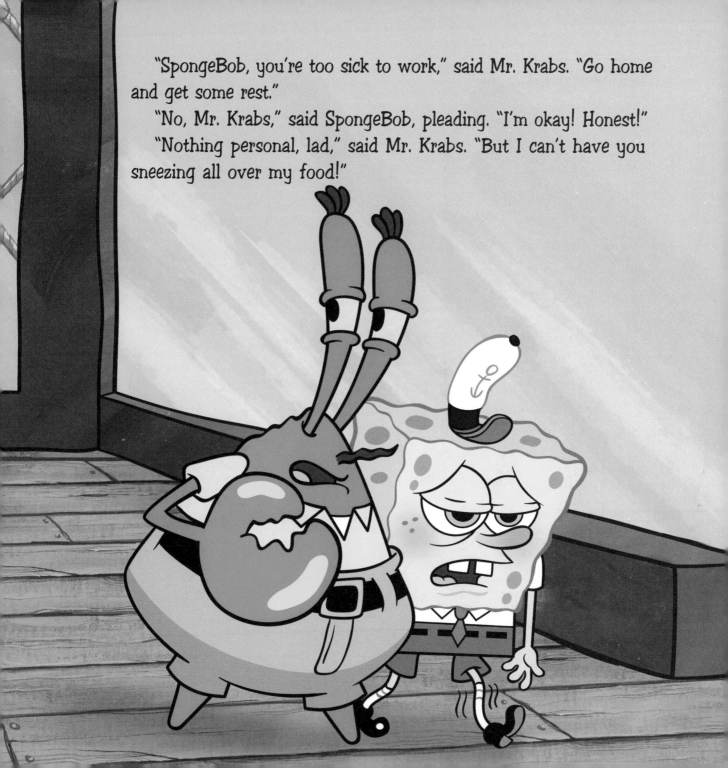

"Who am I kidding, Gary? AH-CHOO! I've got the suds," said SpongeBob sadly. "I'd better go see the doctor before I get worse."

SpongeBob called up his friend Sandy Cheeks. "Sandy, I'm sick. Can you take me to the doctor?"

"Sure, SpongeBob!" said Sandy. "I'll be there faster than you can say 'Sandy, I'm sick. Can you take me to the doctor?'"

"Hey, SpongeBob. Going skiing?" asked Patrick.

"I'm sick, Patrick," said SpongeBob, sniffling. "I'm going to the doctor."

"No!" cried Patrick. "You can't go to the doctor!"

"Why not?" asked SpongeBob.

Patrick pushed SpongeBob back into his house. "I know a guy who knows a guy who went to the doctor's office once. It's a horrible place!"

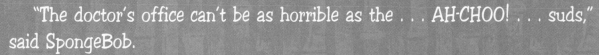
"The doctor's office can't be as horrible as the . . . AH-CHOO! . . . suds," said SpongeBob.

"Yes, it is," said Patrick. "First they make you sit in the . . . *waiting room!*"

"Is that the horrible part?" asked a nervous SpongeBob.

Patrick shook his head. "No! It gets worse! They make you read . . . *old magazines!*"

"Oh, no!" cried SpongeBob. "I'm scared. I don't want to go to the doctor!"

"You've got to help me get better, Patrick," said SpongeBob. "Will you be my doctor?"

Patrick scratched his head. "Well, I didn't go to doctor school, and I don't know anything about medicine, but sure! I'll do it!" Patrick started putting corks into all of SpongeBob's holes. "There. That ought to do the trick!" he said, clapping his hands.

"Do you feel better now, SpongeBob?" asked Patrick.

"I . . . I . . . AH . . . AH . . . AH-CHOO!" SpongeBob sneezed, and he blew up like a balloon. "No bubbles!" said SpongeBob excitedly. "Doctor Patrick, it looks like your treatment is working!"

"I'll send you my bill in the mail," said Patrick.

"I'll be cured in no time," said SpongeBob. "I should call Sandy and tell her she doesn't need to take me to the doctor."

SpongeBob tried to push the buttons on the phone, but his fingers were too big and puffy. "Doctor Patrick, will you call Sandy for me?" he asked.

"Hello, Sandy, this is Doctor Patrick. I'm calling on behalf of my patient, Mr. SquarePants. You don't need to take him to the doctor."

"Patrick, you're not a doctor!" said Sandy. "Tell SpongeBob I'll be there faster than a barefoot jackrabbit in a race!"

"Sandy's coming, and she's bringing a jackrabbit!" cried Patrick.
"You've got to make me well or she'll take me to the doctor!" yelled
SpongeBob.

"I know exactly what to do," said Patrick. He put a giant bandage on SpongeBob's nose, spread jellyfish jelly on his feet, and played a song on the accordion. "Do you feel better?" he asked.

"No!" said SpongeBob. "And Sandy's going to be here any second!"

Sandy pounded on SpongeBob's door. "Open up!" she yelled.

"I'm sorry. There's nobody home," called Patrick.

"Where's SpongeBob?" Sandy asked.

"Uh, he's not here at the moment," said Patrick. "Please leave your message after the beep. *Beep!*"

Sandy karate-chopped the door down. "Patrick, I am taking SpongeBob
to see a real doctor!" She pushed SpongeBob out the door and rolled him
down the road.

"He's fine!" cried Patrick, running after her. "Tell her how fine you are,
SpongeBob!"

"I'm . . . AH-CHOO . . . fine!" said SpongeBob.

SpongeBob started rolling down the hill toward the Krusty Krab!
"SpongeBob, stop!" shouted Mr. Krabs. "You can't come back to work!
You're still sick. Plus, there's no way you'll fit into your uniform now!"

SpongeBob rolled up to the front door and sneezed a giant sneeze.

There was no denying it. SpongeBob needed a *real* doctor.

He went to see the best doctor in Bikini Bottom.

"Well, Mr. SquarePants, you have the suds," said the doctor. "Are you ready for your treatment?"

"Are you going to make me wait in the waiting room and read old magazines?" asked a worried SpongeBob.

The doctor laughed. "No, silly. I'll give you some medicine, and you'll feel all better!"

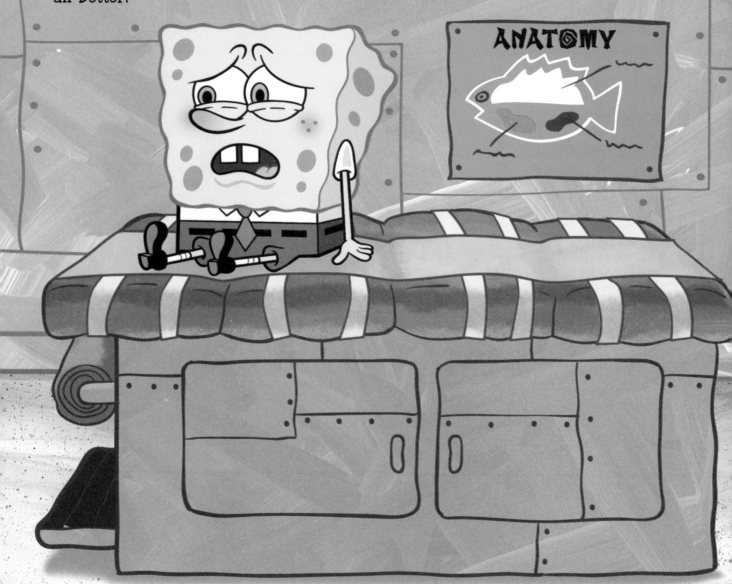

Patrick and Sandy were waiting for SpongeBob in the waiting room.

"SpongeBob, you're all better!" said Sandy. "Aren't you glad you saw the doctor?"

"I sure am!" said SpongeBob. "Hey, Patrick? Are you enjoying that old magazine you're reading?"

Patrick screamed, "Old magazine! NOOOOOOO!" And he ran away as fast as he could!

TENTACLE

D
ONTG
OFORTH
EBAIT

Walrus Journal